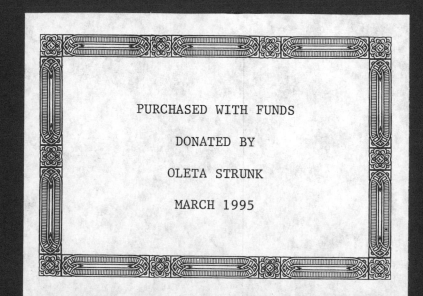

CROW &FOX

AND OTHER ANIMAL LEGENDS

▼ ▼ ▼

JAN THORNHILL

MAR   1995

SIMON & SCHUSTER BOOKS FOR YOUNG READERS
Published by Simon & Schuster
New York   London   Toronto   Sydney   Tokyo   Singapore

The author would like to express her gratitude
to the librarians of Boys and Girls House in Toronto,
to the Ontario Arts Council, and to the storytellers of the world.

SIMON & SCHUSTER BOOKS FOR YOUNG READERS
Simon & Schuster Building, Rockefeller Center
1230 Avenue of the Americas, New York, New York 10020
Copyright ©1993 by Jan Thornhill
Published in Canada by Greey de Pencier Books
SIMON & SCHUSTER BOOKS FOR YOUNG READERS is a trademark of Simon & Schuster.
Designed by Julia Naimska
Manufactured in Hong Kong

10 9 8 7 6 5 4 3 2 1

Library of Congress Cataloging-in-Publication Data
Thornhill, Jan.
Crow & fox and other animal legends / retold and illustrated by Jan Thornhill.
p.   cm. Summary: A collection of traditional tales about animals, from
such parts of the world as India, West Africa, and South America.
1. Tales. 2. Animals—Folklore. [1. Folklore. 2. Animals—Folklore.]
I. Title. PZ8.1.T3794An   1993 398.2—dc20 [E] 93–20205 CIP
ISBN: 0–671–87428–4

INTRODUCTION

While researching this book of animal folktales, I discovered that many of the same stories are shared by people all over the world. Long before they were ever written down, some tales had traveled by way of storytelling over mountain ranges and vast deserts, through rain forests and across oceans. Others may have sprung up like identical flowers in the imaginations of ancient storytellers separated by great distances.

The stories vary in their telling from place to place — sometimes the characters change, or the endings — but the basic stories remain the same. For instance, the Chinese tale I've retold about the tortoise flying with cranes is also told in India, but with a turtle and geese. In Russia, it's a frog and ducks, while in Mexico, it's a snake and vultures.

In choosing the stories for this collection, I traveled around the world in a special way. I began by looking for stories with two animal characters. I then found my way from one continent to another, with one animal character from each story taking me to my next destination. I hope you get as much pleasure from this amazing journey as I did.

ELEPHANT AND HARE

▼ ▼ ▼

A story from India

 HARE AND HER FRIENDS HAD ALWAYS LIVED PEACEFULLY among the tall grasses that grew on the shore of a clear blue lake. No one ever bothered them.

One day Elephant came crashing out of the jungle, followed by his herd. The elephants were thirsty and had been looking for water for a long time. When they saw the shimmering blue lake, they were so excited, they stampeded through the grasses toward the water. They were in such a hurry, they didn't notice that they were trampling the burrows of Hare's friends beneath their huge feet.

After drinking and washing, Elephant led his herd back into the jungle to spend the night. On their way, the elephants' enormous feet crushed many of the tender grasses that Hare and her friends used for food.

Hare was frantic with worry. She knew the elephants would return to the lake the next day, and the hares' homes and food would be destroyed completely. She thought very hard and finally came up with an idea.

"Don't worry," she told the other hares. "I have a plan."

A full moon was just peeking above the trees as Hare hopped to the jungle to talk to Elephant. She hopped right into the middle of the herd and started shouting as loud as she could, but no one paid any attention to her because her voice was tiny and hard for elephants to hear. When Hare was almost hoarse with shouting, Elephant flapped his ears. He thought there was some kind of strange insect buzzing around his head. He flapped his ears again, but the noise wouldn't go away.

"What's that annoying sound?" he finally said.

"It's me!" shouted Hare.

Elephant looked down. He squinted at Hare and said, "Who are you?"

"I am a loyal subject of the all-powerful moon god," said Hare, bowing. "He has sent me to give you a message."

"Go on," said Elephant politely, although he didn't believe a word Hare was saying.

"When you and your herd went down to the lake today," said Hare, trying not to sound nervous, "you trampled the homes and food of the moon god's loyal subjects. This has made the moon god extremely angry. He is so angry that he commands you to leave and never return."

"I don't believe in any moon god," scoffed Elephant. "Give me proof."

"Follow me to the lake then, and you will see the moon god for yourself," said Hare. "But watch where you're walking this time," she added.

When Elephant and Hare got to the edge of the lake, Hare pointed at the reflection of the full moon in the still water.

"There is the mighty moon god," she said. "Pay your respects by dipping your trunk in the lake."

Elephant thought this was a silly thing to do, but he agreed. He stretched out his long trunk and touched the surface of the lake with it. Instantly, the water quivered and rippled, making the moon's reflection burst into hundreds of shimmering pieces. Elephant threw back his trunk in fright.

"See how angry the moon god is?" shouted Hare.

"You're right," said Elephant, shaking with fear. "I promise I'll never annoy the moon god again!"

And with that Elephant headed back to his herd in the jungle, being very careful indeed not to step on any grasses or burrows on his way.

HARE AND TORTOISE

▼ ▼ ▼

A story from West Africa

 THE KING OF ANIMALS HAD A POND IN WHICH NO ONE ELSE was allowed to bathe, not even his family. One night Hare came along. He was hot and dusty, and when he saw the pond, he just jumped right in and washed himself.

The next day the king was outraged to see that someone had muddied his pond. He offered a reward for the intruder's capture.

"I'll catch him," said Tortoise. The king agreed to let her try.

Tortoise got her husband to cover her shell with sticky sap. At sunset she plodded over to the pond, pulled in her legs and head, and waited.

Hare arrived for another bath. "Here's a good rock to rest on," he said, and he sat down on Tortoise's back. Instantly, he stuck to the sap. Tortoise stretched out her neck and feet and started walking toward the king's house.

"This isn't a rock, it's a tortoise!" cried Hare. "Let me go or I'll hit you."

Tortoise kept walking, so Hare thumped her shell hard with his foot. It stuck. He thumped Tortoise with his other foot. It stuck too. Hare hit Tortoise with his left hand, then his right hand. They both stuck.

"Let me go!" he shrieked, and he hit Tortoise with his head. Now even his head was stuck. Tortoise just kept walking, all the way to the king's house.

"Tie Hare up and chop off his head," the king commanded.

After Hare's arms and legs were bound, the king asked if he had a last request. "Yes, I do," said Hare. "I want to die with courage, unbound."

The king thought that was fair and untied him.

Hare smiled slyly. "I thank you, Your Majesty," he said. Then he took an enormous leap and bounded away so fast that no one could catch him!

TORTOISE AND CRANE

▼ ▼ ▼

A story from China

 TORTOISE'S BEST FRIENDS WERE CRANE AND HER BROTHER. They all lived in a beautiful blue lake. There were lots of insects for Tortoise to eat and plenty of frogs and fish for the cranes. Then one year no rain fell. The grasses around the water's edge turned brown. Mud dried up and cracked. The lake got smaller and smaller, and one by one the frogs and fish began to disappear. Crane was worried. One day she waded sadly over to Tortoise.

"There's not enough food here any more for my brother and me," Crane said. "So we've decided to fly off to find another lake. But," she promised, "we'll come back when the rains start."

Tortoise didn't like the idea of being left behind at all. He was already having trouble finding enough insects to fill his belly each day. "Oh, go ahead," he said bitterly. "But when you return, all you'll find here is my empty shell."

Crane decided that she couldn't leave without her friend. Luckily, she had an idea. She found a strong stick at the water's edge and carried it over to Tortoise.

"We can take you with us," said Crane. "All you have to do is grab hold of the middle of this stick with your mouth, and we'll carry you!"

"What a wonderful plan!" Tortoise exclaimed happily.

"There's just one thing you'll have to remember," said Crane. "You can't open your mouth once we're in the air or you'll fall. You can't say anything, not a single word."

"Of course I won't," said Tortoise. "What do you think I am? Stupid?"

So Tortoise latched onto the middle of the stick with his mouth while Crane and her brother each clasped an end with their long bills. The two birds flapped their huge wings and took flight. Tortoise dangled between them, holding the stick tight between his jaws.

After a few minutes, the odd threesome passed over some people working in a rice paddy. One man said to another, "Look at that. What a smart tortoise — he's convinced those birds to carry him in the sky!"

Tortoise heard this and swelled up with pride even though he knew it hadn't been his plan at all. He wanted to shout down to the people, "Yes, I am brilliant, aren't I?" But he remembered just in time how dangerous it would be to open his mouth.

The three flew on, sailing over the countryside. Gradually the flatlands grew into hills, the hills into mountains. Eventually, they passed over a group of children picking tea leaves on a mountainside. One child saw them and pointed them out to her friends. "Oh, what clever birds!" she shouted. "To think of carrying that slow-moving, dim-witted tortoise through the air!"

Tortoise couldn't stand having the children believe it was Crane's idea and not his. Without thinking, he opened his mouth to shout down that he was the smart one. But before Tortoise could get a single word out, he found himself tumbling toward the earth, wind whistling in his ears. With a tremendous thump, he landed on the side of a mountain, cracking his shell so badly that it took months to heal. And since that day, all tortoise shells look as if they've been broken and mended.

CRANE AND CROW

▼ ▼ ▼

A story from Australia

 CRANE WAS A VERY GOOD FISHERMAN. HE WOULD USE HIS feet with their long toes to chase fish out from under rocks and logs in the creek. Then he would snatch the fish up with his long pointed bill. He always caught lots of fish.

One day when he'd gathered a huge number on the bank, Crow came by. She was pure white back then.

"Give me some fish," Crow said hungrily.

"Wait until they're cooked," said Crane. "They're better cooked."

But Crow was impatient and kept pestering Crane for a bite.

"Just wait a minute," snapped Crane, and he turned to tend the fire.

Crow sneaked up to steal one of the fish while Crane wasn't looking. Crane saw Crow out of the corner of his eye and grabbed the fish. He slapped Crow right across the face with it. Crow fell down in the black, charred grass beside the fire. When she got up from the ground, Crow saw that her beautiful white feathers had turned pure black, as they are on all crows to this day.

Even after a week, Crow was still upset about her feathers changing color. She thought it was Crane's fault, so she flew over to the creek where Crane lived. Crane was sleeping. Crow saw a fish bone on the ground and picked it up. Very carefully, she opened Crane's bill and stuck the fish bone down his throat. Then, as quietly as she could, she tiptoed away.

When Crane woke up, he was choking. He tried to cough up the bone in his throat, but all that came out was a scraping, croaking sound. And that scraping croak is still the only sound Crane and his children can make.

CROW AND FOX

▼ ▼ ▼

A story from the Middle East

 FOX INVITED HIS RIVAL, CROW, TO DINNER. CROW SAID HE'D be honored to come, so Fox set to work preparing a porridge made with flour and camel's milk.

"Welcome, Crow," said Fox when Crow arrived. Fox then poured the food onto a flat rock. "Help yourself to as much as you can eat," he said.

Crow pecked at the porridge with his beak but couldn't get even a single mouthful of food off the rock. Meanwhile, Fox noisily lapped up every last dribble of porridge with his long pink tongue.

Crow thought Fox was an incredibly rude host, but he didn't say anything. Instead, he invited Fox to a feast of ripe dates the very next day. Fox began to drool and lick his chops. He hardly ever had a chance to eat sweet, ripe dates because they grow high up at the very top of palm trees.

"Welcome, Fox," said Crow when Fox appeared at his house. Crow flew up into a date palm and began picking off the ripest, sweetest dates with his beak. One by one he dropped them into a thick, prickly thornbush growing at the base of the palm tree.

"Eat!" he shouted down to Fox. "Eat until you can't eat any more!"

Fox circled the bush, trying to get at the dates, but every time he poked his snout in to grab one between his teeth, his nose was pricked by thorns. Crow flew down to a branch above Fox's head and began feasting on the dates, plucking them easily from the thornbush with his thick, hard beak.

Fox slunk away with an empty stomach. From then on, he never treated a guest rudely again.

FOX AND BEAR

▼ ▼ ▼

A story from Northern Europe

 ONE COLD WINTER DAY, BEAR MET FOX, WHO WAS DRAGGING behind her a long line of fish she'd stolen.

"Where did you find those lovely fish?" asked Bear, licking her lips and swishing her tail. This was back when Bear had a long, bushy tail she was very proud of.

"You mean these?" asked Fox, lifting the line so the fish sparkled in the sun. "I went fishing and caught them."

Now, bears are very fond of fish, so Bear asked Fox if she would share her catch.

"No," said Fox. "I need them all for myself."

"How can I catch my own then?" Bear asked.

"Oh, it's easy," said Fox. "All you have to do is cut a hole in the ice, put your tail in the water, and wait. Lots of fish will grab onto it."

So Bear went off to the river, cut a hole in the ice with her powerful claws, and put her tail in. After a while, her tail began to sting, but Bear thought it was just fish latching on with their sharp little teeth. As the hours passed, it hurt more and more, but Bear didn't move because she wanted to catch lots of fish. Finally, when the ache went all the way up to her head, Bear decided she'd caught enough for one day. She tried to pull her tail out, but it wouldn't budge. Bear's tail had frozen solid into the ice. Fox had tricked her. Bear pulled and pulled, but her tail was really stuck.

"You rascal, Fox!" she yelled, still pulling.

Then, with one mighty tug, her tail snapped right off. That's why bears all over the world have short, stubby tails to this very day.

BEAR AND COYOTE

▼ ▼ ▼

A story from Western Canada

 LONG AGO, BEFORE THERE WAS NIGHT AND DAY, GRIZZLY Bear and Coyote shared the same tepee. The two of them were having a contest to decide whether it would be night all the time or day all the time. Grizzly Bear wanted night, Coyote wanted day.

"Night, night, night," said Grizzly Bear.

"Day, day, day," said Coyote.

The one who said his choice the most times inside the tepee would win.

"I know how to keep Grizzly Bear out of the tepee for a long time," Coyote said to himself.

Coyote went out to a log that Grizzly Bear liked to sit on. The log lay across a deep ravine. Coyote told the worms in the log to chew until the wood was almost chewed right through. Then he went back to the tepee and lay down.

"Day, day, day," said Coyote for a long time.

"Night, night, night," said Grizzly Bear for a long time.

Grizzly Bear was tired of being in the tepee and decided to take a break. He went outside to his favorite log. Halfway across he sat down. The log broke and Grizzly Bear fell into the ravine. While he was slowly climbing out, Grizzly Bear figured out that Coyote must have had something to do with his fall. So he went to the lake, built a fire, and warmed up some water. He put some stinky medicine in the water and had a bath. Then he went back to the tepee.

"Night, night, night," said Grizzly Bear.

"Day, day...Whew!" said Coyote, sniffing. "Something smells terrible! You must have stepped in something, Grizzly Bear."

Grizzly Bear looked at the bottoms of his paws. "There's nothing on my paws," he said.

"Well, something really stinks," said Coyote, but he didn't leave the tepee.

Grizzly Bear went back down to the lake and had another medicine bath to make himself smell even worse. Then he went back to the tepee. He expected Coyote to be chased out by the smell.

Coyote plugged his nose when Grizzly Bear sat down. "You'd better go wipe your paws, Grizzly Bear," said Coyote. "You smell really, really bad."

"I don't smell anything," said Grizzly Bear. He lay down and tried to think of another way to make Coyote stay out of the tepee.

"Night, night, night," said Grizzly Bear.

"Day, day, day," said Coyote.

Coyote got an idea before Grizzly Bear and went outside again. He hurried along the shore of the lake, gathering dried fish bones. He threw them in the water. "When Grizzly Bear comes," he told the bones, "jump up out of the water as if you're trying to catch flies."

Coyote went back to the tepee.

"Night, night, night," said Grizzly Bear.

"While you're wasting time saying 'Night, night, night,'" said Coyote, "there are hundreds of fish jumping in the lake."

"Fish!" said Grizzly Bear. He ran out of the tepee and down to the lake, where he saw many fish jumping. He tried to catch them, but they disappeared whenever he got close because they weren't really fish, they were just bones.

Grizzly Bear gave up and went back to the tepee.

"Day, day, day," Coyote was saying.

"Night, night, night," Grizzly Bear joined in.

The contest went on for a long time. Sometimes Coyote got the best of Grizzly Bear, other times Grizzly Bear got the best of Coyote, but in the end it was a tie.

That's why today we have both day and night.

COYOTE AND MOUSE

▼ ▼ ▼

A story from the American Southwest

 A LONG TIME AGO THE ONLY WAY TO MAKE COYOTE LAUGH was to call him Yellow Behind the Ears. This was supposed to be a secret, but Mouse found out somehow. She decided to play a trick on Coyote. Mouse hid in a pile of rocks beside the path Coyote always used when he went to the spring to get water for his children. Sure enough, after a little while Coyote trotted by. He came back a minute later, his cheeks bulging with water. That's how Coyote carries water back to his children in their den. When he came alongside the rock pile, Mouse called out, "Yellow Behind the Ears! Yellow Behind the Ears!"

Coyote stopped dead in his tracks and started laughing the way coyotes laugh. He had to spit his mouthful of water on the ground.

"Who made me laugh?" he yelled. "You won't get away with it! I'm Coyote!"

Coyote ran back to the spring and filled his mouth with water again. And again when he passed the rock pile, Mouse called out, "Yellow Behind the Ears! Yellow Behind the Ears!"

Coyote couldn't help himself. He had to laugh. Out sputtered the water again. This made Coyote really angry.

"Whoever you are, you'll be sorry!" he yelled. "You won't get away with making me have to go back to the spring again!" Coyote started looking for whoever was making him laugh, but he couldn't find anybody. Mouse was really tiny. She was hidden between two big rocks, giggling. She giggled quietly so Coyote wouldn't hear her.

Coyote went off for water again. When he came back up the path, Mouse called out, "Yellow Behind the Ears! Yellow Behind the Ears!"

Now Coyote was furious, but there was nothing he could do. He just had to laugh. It was so incredibly funny. He spit out his water again and laughed so hard he almost burst.

"Who is making me laugh?" Coyote shouted. "You're in big trouble, whoever you are!" He ran from rock to rock, sticking his nose in crevices and sniffing and snorting. But still he couldn't find anybody. Mouse was rolling around in her hiding place, laughing so hard she had to hold her sides.

Grumbling to himself, Coyote went back for water a fourth time. As he lapped up yet another mouthful, he told himself that if he heard the name Yellow Behind the Ears again, he'd hold his lips so tight together that he wouldn't be able to laugh. But when he passed the rock pile and Mouse called out "Yellow Behind the Ears! Yellow Behind the Ears!" Coyote's lips wouldn't stay closed. Out came the water. Coyote laughed so loud and so hard this time that he could be heard far across the desert.

By now Coyote was frantic with anger. "I'll find you!" he cried. He circled the rock pile three times. He poked his nose into every crack and cranny trying to pick up a scent, but Mouse was well hidden at the bottom of the rock pile.

Coyote couldn't figure it out. Why couldn't he find anybody?

"Maybe it's a ghost," Coyote thought suddenly. "Are you a ghost?" he said out loud. There was no answer.

Coyote went for water a fifth time, thinking nervously, "It's a ghost. What else could it be? It must be a ghost." This time when he came back, he made a wide circle around the rocks.

Mouse peeked out from her hiding place. She was about to gleefully call out "Yellow Behind the Ears" when she saw that Coyote's tail was between his legs. Coyote looked so frightened and nervous that Mouse felt sorry for him. This time she didn't shout anything at all, she just let Coyote pass with his mouth full of water for his children.

MOUSE AND TAPIR

▼ ▼ ▼

A story from South America

 LONG, LONG AGO, EVERYBODY WAS HUNGRY. THERE WAS never much food around and what there was to eat tasted like nothing at all. Only Tapir was fat. Every day she'd go off into the forest for hours at a time. Sometimes when she returned, she smelled like something sweet. Other times she would burp. Mouse began to get suspicious and called a meeting of all the other animals and birds.

"Tapir's finding something good to eat, and she's not sharing it with us," said Mouse.

"We'll follow her tomorrow," someone suggested.

"Mouse should go alone," said someone else. "He's the smallest. Tapir won't see him."

So it was decided.

When Tapir set off into the forest the next morning, Mouse scurried quietly after her. After a very long walk, Mouse saw Tapir enter a clearing. When Mouse got closer, he couldn't believe his eyes. In the middle of the clearing was an enormous tree, the biggest tree in the world. It had hundreds of huge branches, and each branch was heavy with foods Mouse had never seen before — ripe bananas and plantains, mangoes and papayas, squashes and corn, pumpkins and pomegranates, sweet potatoes and yams — all kinds of edible things. It was the Food Tree.

And there was Tapir, greedily eating the ripe fruits that had fallen to the ground.

Mouse hurried back to the village to tell the others what he had

▼ ▼ ▼ 28 ▼ ▼ ▼

discovered. They all stopped what they were doing and followed Mouse to the Food Tree. Tapir was lying at its base, still eating. Even her chin hairs were dripping with juice.

"Why didn't you tell us about this tree?" asked Mouse. But Tapir didn't answer. She just grunted.

Most of the food was too high to reach, so everyone gathered in a circle to decide what to do. They were all so hungry, they had no choice but to cut down the tree. They began right away, the birds pecking with their beaks and the animals digging with their claws and gnawing with their teeth at the massive trunk. Tapir didn't help at all. She was too full to move.

Finally, after two whole days and two whole nights of work, the Food Tree swayed for a moment, then tottered. There was a deafening *crunch* as the Food Tree began to fall. Broken branches laden with fruit came tumbling down. When the gigantic trunk hit the ground, the whole world shook.

After everything had settled, the birds and animals gathered again. Mouse noticed that where a banana branch had fallen, several banana trees had sprouted in the ground. Banana trees had never existed before. Tapir pointed out some corn growing a short distance away. There had never been corn plants before. Fruits and vegetables that had never grown anywhere but on the Food Tree were suddenly growing everywhere.

The fruits of the Food Tree still grow to this very day, food for all the animals and people of the world.

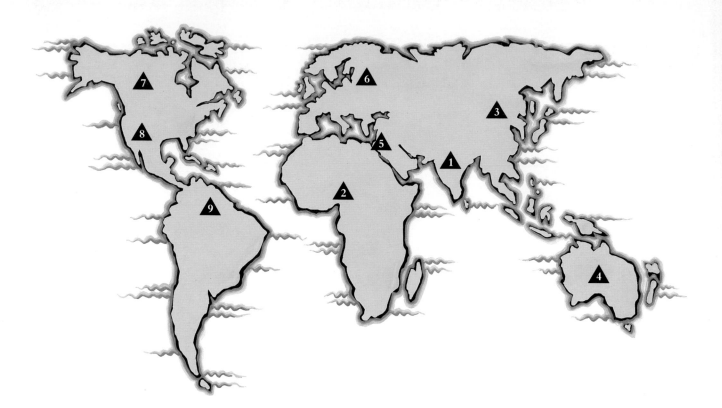

1. INDIA *Elephant and Hare*
Border based on Indian fabric design

2. WEST AFRICA *Hare and Tortoise*
Border based on African blanket design

3. CHINA *Tortoise and Crane*
Border based on Chinese imperial robe

4. AUSTRALIA *Crane and Crow*
Border based on Aborigine bark paintings

5. MIDDLE EAST *Crow and Fox*
Border based on Egyptian carpet

6. NORTHERN EUROPE *Fox and Bear*
Border based on Norwegian knitting

7. WESTERN CANADA *Bear and Coyote*
Border based on Sioux beadwork

8. AMERICAN SOUTHWEST *Coyote and Mouse*
Border based on ancient Anasazi pottery

9. SOUTH AMERICA *Mouse and Tapir*
Border based on Waurá body painting